I CAN HELP!

No part of this publication may be reproduced, stored in a retrieval system, or transmitted in any form or by any means, electronic, mechanical, photocopying, recording, or otherwise, without written permission of the publisher. For information regarding permission, write to Scholastic Inc., Attention: Permissions Department, 557 Broadway, New York, NY 10012.

Copyright © 1997 by Hans Wilhelm, Inc.

All rights reserved. Published by Scholastic Inc.
SCHOLASTIC, CARTWHEEL BOOKS, NOODLES, and associated logos
are trademarks and/or registered trademarks of Scholastic Inc.
Lexile is a registered trademark of MetaMetrics, Inc.

Library of Congress Cataloging-in-Publication Data is available.

ISBN-13: 978-0-439-46621-9
ISBN-10: 0-439-46621-0

17 16 15 14 13 12 11   09 10 11 12

Printed in the U.S.A. 23 • This edition first printing, June 2009

SCHOLASTIC READER
LEVEL 1
50-250 WORDS

I CAN HELP!

by Hans Wilhelm

Cartwheel
·B·O·O·K·S·®

SCHOLASTIC INC.
New York Toronto London Auckland
Sydney Mexico City New Delhi Hong Kong

Today, I play grown-up.

I can help Baby.

Oops!

I can help clean.

Oh, no!

I can help plant.

Oops!

I can't do anything.
I'm useless.

Why are grown-ups so smart?

They must have made
many mistakes, too.

They just didn't quit.
And neither will I!

Come here, Baby.
Let me help you.

I am very careful.

See? I can help!

Boom!